This book
belongs to

....

For Betsy, who means something special to me —V. X. K.

Published by Bloomsbury Books for Young Readers
175 Fifth Avenue, New York, New York 10010

Library of Congress Cataloging-in-Publication Data
Kirsch, Vincent X.
Two little boys from Toolittle Toys / by Vincent X. Kirsch. — 1st U.S. ed.
p.   cm.
Summary: The Toolittle Toy Company makes toys that children like
to play with by making toys that like to play with children.
ISBN 978-1-59990-428-3 (hardcover)
[1. Toys—Fiction. 2. Brothers—Fiction.] I. Title.
PZ7.K6383Tw 2010   [E]—dc22   2009034583

Art created with watercolor wash and graphite and
colored pencil on hot pressed watercolor paper
Typeset in Century Expanded
Book design by Vincent X. Kirsch and Donna Mark

First U.S. Edition August 2010
Printed in China by Hung Hing (China) Co., Ltd, Shenzhen, Guangdong
1 2 3 4 5 6 7 8 9 10

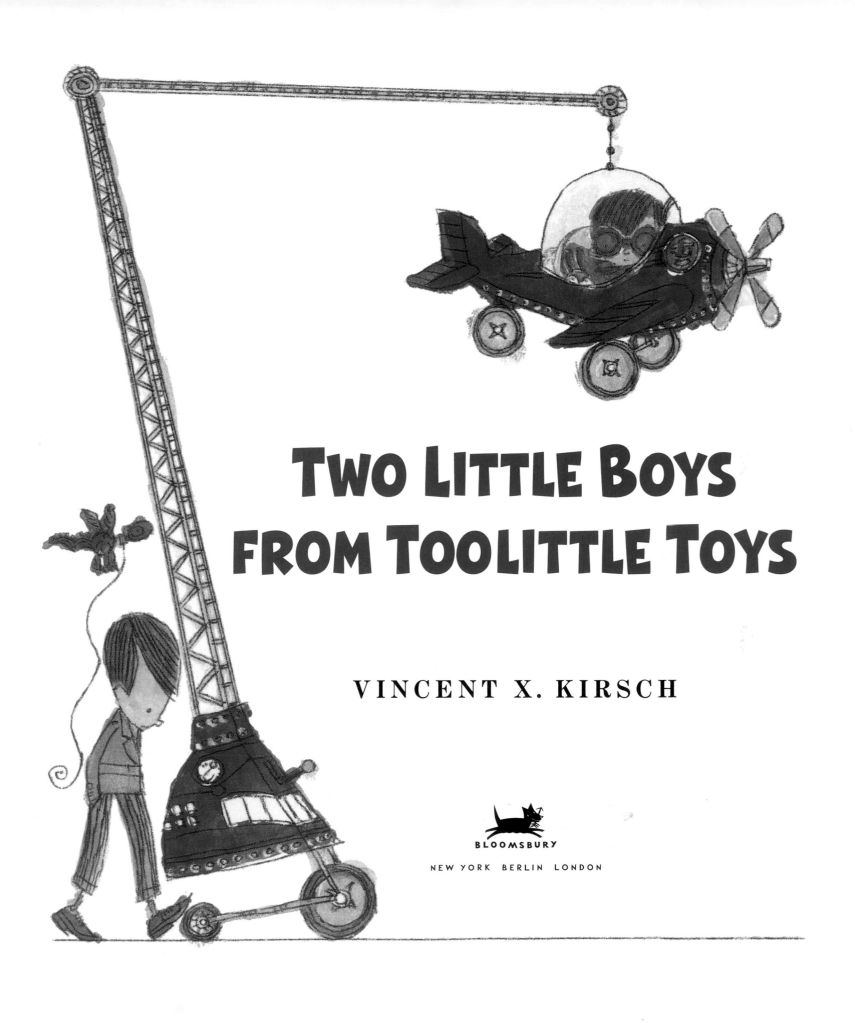

TWO LITTLE BOYS
FROM TOOLITTLE TOYS

VINCENT X. KIRSCH

BLOOMSBURY

NEW YORK BERLIN LONDON

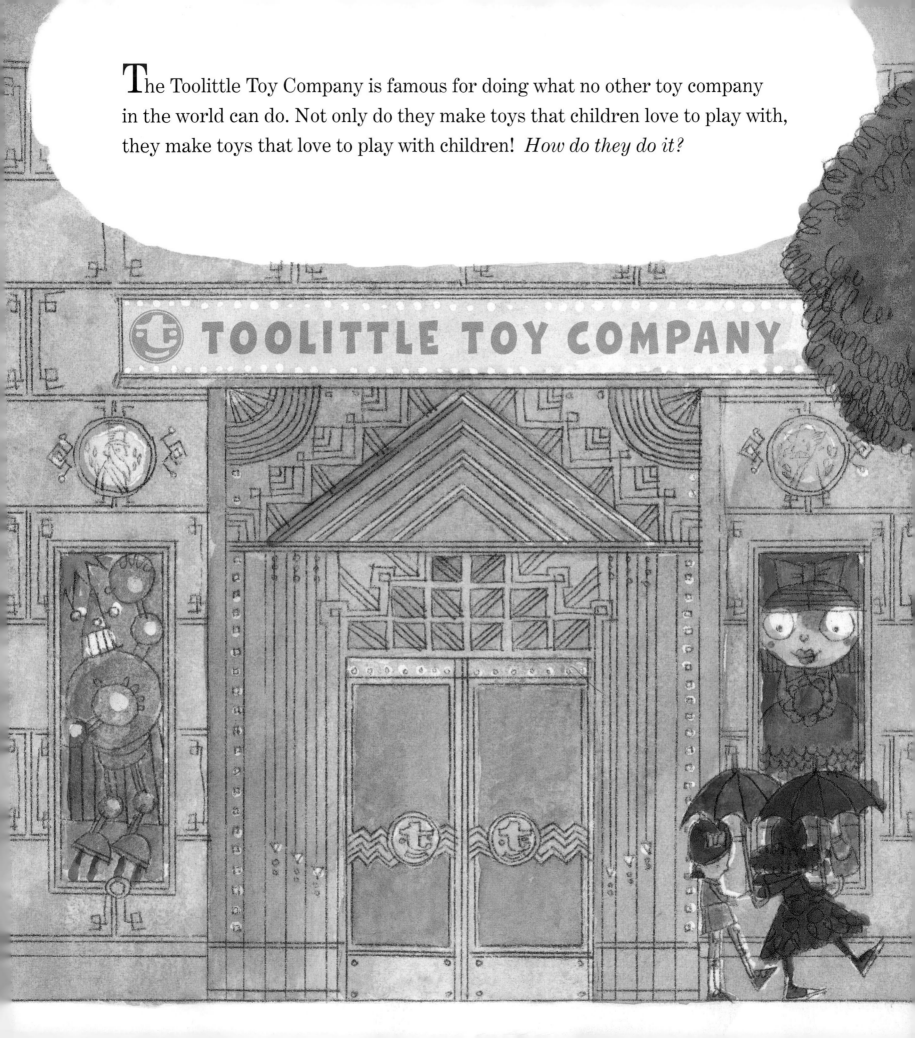

The Toolittle Toy Company is famous for doing what no other toy company in the world can do. Not only do they make toys that children love to play with, they make toys that love to play with children! *How do they do it?*

TOOLITTLE TOY COMPANY

The secret is little Rudy Toolittle and his littler brother, Ridley.
Every Saturday morning, brand-new toys are waiting for them in
the Toolittle toy laboratories. By Monday morning, the boys must try
out each new toy to make absolutely sure every one is playing perfectly.

One Saturday Rudy said to his little brother, "I am getting too big to play with toys. It is time for me to take toys seriously." After all, he was too big to fit inside the two-seat Toolittle V.I.P. Hiwire-Hiflyer like he used to.

To show that he meant it, Rudy gave Ridley his favorite toy and said, "You can play by yourself."

Since the Toolittle toys were not ordinary toys, they could hardly wait to start playing. The trouble was, Ridley didn't want to play all by himself.

Rudy got right to work, taking toys seriously. He organized, measured, and numbered every Toolittle toy he could find. The toys had to wait their turn.

Ridley waited too.

Rudy studied diagrams and read instruction manuals from cover to cover.

"Could I read about the toys too?" Ridley asked.
Rudy knew better. Ridley was too little to read.
"Please be quiet," Rudy whispered.

Next, Rudy took the toys apart
to see how they worked.

"I know how the toys work," Ridley said. "Let me help!"

Rudy knew better. Ridley was too little to know such things. So Rudy gave his brother a handful of knobs, buttons, and cranks to keep him out of the way.

The Toolittle toys were in a zillion bits and pieces. As it turned out, Rudy was much better at taking toys apart than he was at putting them back together.

"I'll help fix the toys, and then we can play!" Ridley said.

Rudy knew better. Ridley was too little to help and was becoming a very big nuisance.

"I have everything under control!" Rudy scolded. "Just leave me alone."

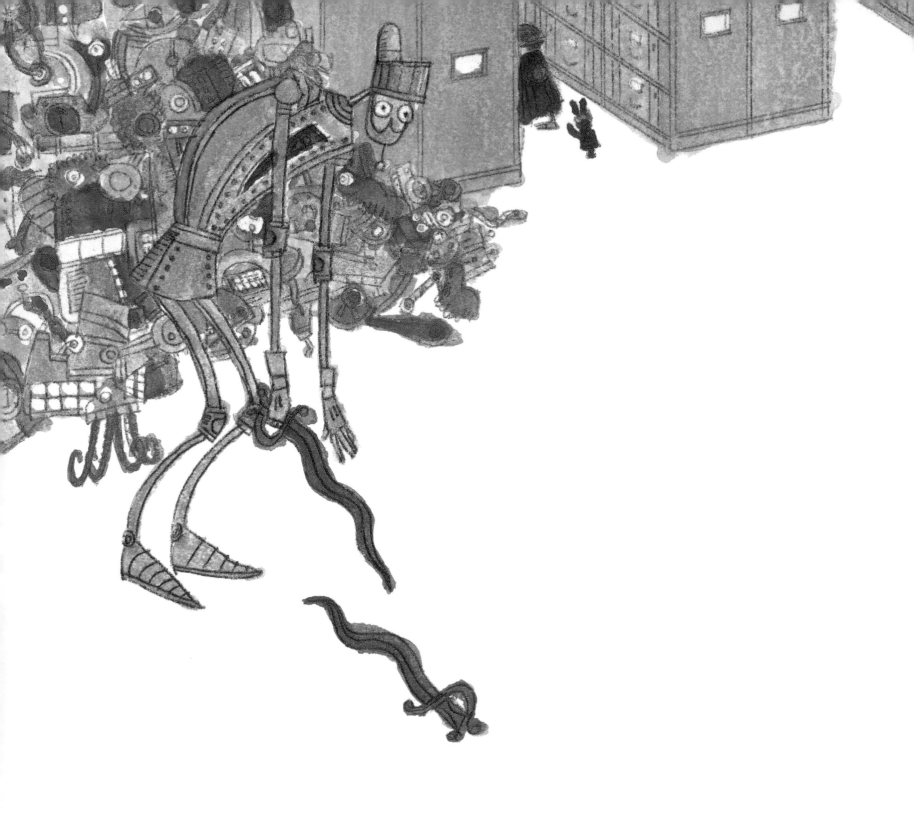

But Rudy did not have everything under control. He challenged a
Robot-in-Shining-Armor to a duel, but it would not fight. He wound up
a tiny one-wheeled Whirli-Whizz, but it would not whirl. No matter
what Rudy did, the toys would not play anymore.

Ridley knew just what to do.

A few minutes later, a toy zigzagged up to Rudy and said, "I am the Toolittle Zigzagging Giggle-Wiggler reporting for duty. I see that you are trying to play with the toys. I can help you put them back together!"

The toy reached into a pocket and pulled out a handful of knobs, buttons, and cranks.

Together, Rudy and the Giggle-Wiggler matched up each piece to the right toy . . . and it worked!

The Giggle-Wiggler and the other Toolittle toys were ready to play. But Rudy was not. "Something is missing," he said.

The Giggle-Wiggler pulled Rudy's favorite toy out from under his hat. "Is this what you are looking for?" he asked.

Even with his favorite toy by his side, Rudy still felt something was missing. Maybe he really was too big to play.

The Toolittle Zigzagging Giggle-Wiggler knew better.

"There you are, Ridley!" Rudy exclaimed happily. "The toys and I are ready to play! Where have you been?"

There wasn't time for Ridley to answer. The two brothers had to get to work right away! They only had until Monday morning to make absolutely sure that each new toy was playing perfectly.

After all, the Toolittle Toy Company is famous for doing
what no other toy company in the world can do. . . .
And the secret is not one but two little Toolittles.

THE TOOLITTLE TOY COMPANY CATALOG

THE TOOLITTLE
TOY COMPANY

SILLY WIZARD WAND KIT
Create your own magic wand
with adjustable spell bands.

PETAL PETS
These perfect pets stay put! Kitten,
puppy, or rabbit sold separately.

POPCORN POPPER ROCKET
Make your own
out-of-this-world popcorn.

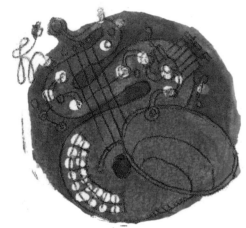

NO-MORE-NOISE-A-FONE
Turns noise into beautiful music.
Requires four hands to operate.

FUNNY FRAME
Show your friends what
you *really* look like!

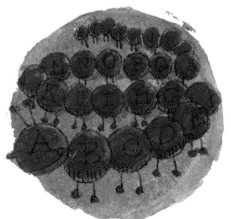

ALPHABETSY
Don't let the ABCs
bug you anymore!

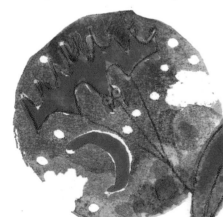

NITE-BRITE BAT KITE
Scare your friends with this
glow-in-the-dark kite.

ATTACHABLE FLOATING FISHTAIL
Feel like a fish in and out of the water.

BUBBLE GUM GUN
The best bubble-blowing gun ever made.
(Bubble gum bullets included!)

Can you
find these
hidden toys in
the story?